H. C Winton

Glen Sketches

H. C Winton

Glen Sketches

ISBN/EAN: 9783337379001

Printed in Europe, USA, Canada, Australia, Japan

Cover: Foto ©Andreas Hilbeck / pixelio.de

More available books at **www.hansebooks.com**

GLEN SKETCHES,

AT HAVANA, N. Y.,

WITH DESCRIPTIVE POEMS.

"The glen, the glen—the silent glen!
Oh, how I love its solitude!"—NEALE.

BY H. C. WINTON.

ITHACA, N. Y.:
ANDRUS, McCHAIN & CO., STEAM PRINTERS.
1868.

CONTENTS.

SECTIONS OF THE GLEN.

PREFACE.

It is hoped that the following pages may merit the approbation of the visitors and admirers of the Glen.

Should they receive sufficient encouragement, it is not improbable that a larger work may be issued at some future time, embellished with copious illustrations.

The general public, who are not familiar with the Glen—its rocky paths, giant cliffs, sparkling cascades, and diversified scenery, in short, with the majesty and beauty of Nature which is here so lavishly displayed—will perhaps regard the descriptive portions of this work in the light of an introduction, as they are merely designed to point out some of the more remarkable features of this interesting summer resort. Should the visitor or tourist, while pausing to admire the wondrous beauty and sublimity of this natural Labyrinthian Gorge, or while reclining beneath the umbrageous foliage of the Glen, find in this little volume a source of pleasure or information, then it will not have been written in vain.

The few fragments of history, of incidents connected with days that are past, which are interwoven in portions of these desultory sketches concerning the Seneca Lake region, it is hoped may not be found entirely devoid of interest, either to the general reader, the tourist; or to the excursionists, so many of whom cross the sparkling waves of the ever beauteous Seneca, in visiting the giens and cascades of the romantic valley, extending from its head waters towards the broad intervales of the Chemung and the Susquehanna.

The limits of this work will not permit of much that might be interesting, perhaps, concerning the aboriginal occupation and pioneer settlements of this region, once the western frontier. The writer, however, has for some time been engaged in collecting materials, and has already in an advanced stage of preparation various extended sketches, which in due time may appear.

SENECA LAKE.

BY J. B. LOOK.

Thou crystal mirror, clear and bright,
　Where red men rode in their bark canoe
Thou ming'lest with the moon's pale light,
　Thy requiem seems a fond adieu;
The "pale face," now, glides o'er thy crest;
　The red man was compelled to flee;
I sit and gaze upon thy breast—
　O, whisper not farewell to me.

I read thy legends long of yore,
　They seem to whisper yet to me;
But now I see thy rock-bound shore,
　Where wild men bent their savage knee.
Thy every breath brings fresh perfume,
　Thy flowers are touched with heavenly dies;
Thou seem'st to all my sight consume;
　I'm basking now between two skies.

The brooklets flow askance the hill,
　And seem to leap to mingle there;
Thou seem'st to beckon to each rill,
　I hear thy whisper on the air.
Near to thy sides the forest groves
　Are talking back in cadence clear;
I linger 'round thy sleeping caves,
　My sight is lost through charms of ear.

O, silv'ry lake, I'd sing to thee
　The sweetest cadence of my song
Thou ling'rest yet in dreams with me,
　I would thy mem'ry still prolong.
But Percival once touched his lyre,
　And breathed thee an undying name,
He set my sluggish soul on fire,
　And made me pant for writing fame.

GENERAL OBSERVATIONS.

WITHIN the limits of the Empire State many rare specimens of Natural Scenery are found.

While some of them are more striking or magnificent than others, they all furnish boundless themes for the imagination of the writer, numerous subjects for the pencil of the artist, and a source of never ending delight to the beholder.

Each new candidate for public favor, each new locality of natural scenic interest, invites more or less attention as its peculiarities or originalities, if we may be allowed the word in this sense, become notorious.

Like many other important natural attractions in Western New York, the wild and startling scenery of the locality of which these pages are to speak—McClure's Glen—a beautiful mountainous ravine in the Seneca Lake Region, to be appreciated needs a personal inspection. Nothing less can satisfy the imagination or give to the reader much more than a faint idea of what it really is, to say nothing of the inadequacy of any or all attempts to portray with pencil or pen the magnificent beauties of the world around us.

At each successive step the beholder seems to turn a fresh page in the book of Nature, engraven as it were in the rocky tablets of this singular ravine ;—the volume bound in blue and green, the cerulean sky above our heads, and the dense foliage heavily embroidering the towering cliffs which are every where visible, from its unpretending commencement in the vale to its summit hundreds of feet above. These, taken together with the undulating evergreens when moved by the passing summer breeze; the unceasing music of the restless waters leaping from rock to rock, combined with the roar of the reverberating cascades; the strains of the feathered songsters which are heard in the recesses of the surrounding forests; the alternate lights and shadows mirrored upon the surface of the numerous pools and water-courses of the Glen, may explain the reason why this quiet retreat presents such rare attractions to the solitary student of Nature or the votaries of pleasure, who are so frequently seen tracing its winding pathways.

It may perhaps be a matter of no little surprise, that arrangements were not long since made so that the Glen might have been accessible. This has been owing to various circumstances; and while the few have been aware of the peculiar channel made by the action of this singular stream, in its course from the Tamarac Swamp among the hills of the town of Catharine, while madly plunging and tumbling from the Seneca Lake Highlands, in their seeming haste to reach, via. the Lake and its outlet, the broad waters of Lake Ontario, from thence to mingle through the River St. Lawrence in the vast bosom of the Atlantic—until quite recently the great natural beauties which for centuries have here been gradually developing, have been almost entirely hidden away from the public gaze. It has been comparatively almost totally unknown, or at least known and explored by the few, so formidable were the natural barriers or obstacles presented in its passage.

Previous to the summer of 1867, at which time the Glen

was opened to the public, by means of paths, stairways, bridges, etc., he who would have sought to examine its hidden recesses, would have found that many valuable requisites generally supposed to be possessed by a skillful or daring topographical engineer, would not have come amiss, either in his mental or physical organization.

The means at present for exploring the entire Glen, although not yet perfected, are such that with ordinary caution a ramble through it may be regarded a safe one. As the work of making the pathways, etc., progresses, improvements in their construction will undoubtedly be suggested, which may tend to lessen the fatigue of the journey and also give an opportunity to pass certain points, which may afford better views of some portion of the ravine, which in the haste that characterized the primary labors of opening the Glen, may have escaped due attention. Besides, as the first paths and structures were made when the volume of the stream was very low, it is quite probable that Dame Nature will point out at times of high water, and in a manner not to be misunderstood, changes which will be needed in the location of bridges and stairways in this portion of her dominions. Some of these changes at present are evident, yet we are reminded of the old adage that " Rome was not built in a day." In this connection it may be mentioned, that in the month of July, 1867, when the sound of the workman's hammer was first heard in the Glen, the work was carried on with almost astonishing rapidity, by the efforts of the citizens of Havana, prominent among whom were the members of Myrtle Lodge, No. 131, F. & A. M.

Less than four days of the combined and voluntary labors of the many willing hands engaged in the enterprise, were required to render the first section of the Glen accessible, including the means of ascending the airy heights of Eagle Cliff Falls and the approaches to the Curtain Cascade, in the spacious amphitheatre above. The undertaking, stimulated by the enthusiasm of its inherent novelty was continued, and soon the triple staircase was completed through the Central Gorge, and the bridge erected across the stream just above. This was the last artificial structure erected in 1867. For convenience and entire safety other structures and paths are needed, but in ordinary seasons the present ones are sufficient, with slight improvements or repairs, to render the passage of the Glen completely feasible. Although its opening incurred considerable effort and expense, no admission fees are charged.

Each season has its peculiar charms in the Glen, but to the generality of people perhaps, the summer is the most delightful time in which to make the visit. The cascades, however, are on some accounts, seen at a much greater advantage immediately after the heavy spring or autumnal rains.

The visitor, while enjoying the cool shades and gentle breezes of the Glen in June or July, may perhaps imagine the "situation" when the stream is vastly swollen, or how the rocks and cliffs must appear when firmly bound in winter's cold embrace, festooned with massive icy pendants glittering beneath an effulgent noon-day sun. In the autumn, also, when the forest leaves are turning to a scarlet hue, the scene is beautifully grand; one by one silently falling, some borne along by the ceaseless water's flow, others wafted here and there at the sport of the wind. Then all Nature proclaims that the brief season is ending. the fleeting year drawing to its close; that when another bright spring-time shall approach, the trees shall commence to put on new robes of green, the smiling rocks, purified by the lingering departure of the melting ice and snow, shall present fresh beauties to her welcome visitants, some of whom will doubtless ramble along the paths ere the first violets of spring have presented their tiny buds, or even dared to peep from their lowly beds.

Some of the visitors who may easily leap across the stream at various points, in the summer season, know but little of the vast torrents of rushing and foaming waters, which course along through this ravine during the time of great freshets. Sometimes large trees are uprooted, and huge boulders of rock are displaced and carried downwards, by the seething flood. Some of the effects of these periodical risings of the waters, may be seen in the channel of the stream both at the entrance of the Glen, and in the varied and romantic passages in the ascent from the Portal Cascade, to the Witches' Caldron, situated in the midst of Central Gorge.

In other respects besides its gorgeous scenery, the Glen is interesting. Geologically considered, the rocks principally belong to the Chemung Group, and among their shale and sandstone formations, much is found to engage the attention of the lover of Natural History. Sulphur Salts, formed by the decomposing shales, are occasionally observed,—a short distance above the Eagle-Cliff Falls, they exude from the rocks in small quantities near the water's edge. The soil about the entrance of the Glen is diversified in its nature, and abounds in pure living springs. Along the rocky avenues there exist also, many curious specimens of the vegetable kingdom, some of which are peculiar to this locality.

During the opening season of the Glen, numerous pic-nic

parties were held in the groves near its entrance. The largest one was attended Sept. 18th, 1867—a Grand Masonic Pic-nic and Festival. Large numbers of the Order, and others, were present, from various sections of the State.

The Pic-nic was one of much interest, and furnished a day long to be remembered in the annals of the Glen. In a letter of Jas. G. Clark, the Poet Vocalist, who attended, to the Utica Morning *Herald*, we find the following : "A person once seeing this spot can never forget it, and this sight is well worth a journey from Utica to Havana. There were, perhaps, 5,000 persons present at the pic-nic—some say 10,000—and the majority of them explored the Glen."

The Corning *Democrat* also remarks—" The Masonic Pic-Nic at Havana, on Wednesday, for the benefit of The Peoples College, was eminently successful. An immense crowd of people was present. The cities of New York and Elmira sent their thousands, escorted by bands, and the country around was well represented. * * * A fine grove at the mouth of McClure's Glen, was the scene of the Pic-Nic—a gay and enlivenng scene it was, too, with groups scattered here and there, discussing the contents of their baskets, the beauties of the Glen and grove, the promises for the success of the Institution, which it had now become the pride of the " mystic band " to complete, establish and perpetuate. "

The Excursion or Pic-nic parties generally bring refreshments or lunches with them, which frequently add much to the comfort or enjoyment of such occasions. As a matter of course, these parties include large proportions of those who know so well how to prepare a dainty sandwich or a tempting dish of tongue. Parties, especially from a distance, usu-ally partake of their repasts in the grove—where convenient tables are always in readiness, the incidental delay affording an opportunity for refreshing rest, which is quite desirable to prepare for the ascent of the ravine. The arrangements are such, however, that refreshments can always be obtained at the buildings near the entrance of the Glen, where also any articles of apparel or incumbrance may be left, which are not particularly needed during the ramble. Parties wishing any souvenirs of the locality can here also obtain fine Stere-oscopic Views of the Glen, by which means the visitor, al-though at a distance, may afterwards, perhaps pleasantly, while away some leisure hour.

Visitors generally—more especially the ladies—will do well to come prepared with suitable dresses, which in making the journey are very desirable, as far as comfort, safety, and economy are concerned.

The Glen, in a public point of view, is yet comparatively in its infancy. Time must show in what manner it will be re-garded ; but thus far, there seem no lack of indications that its celebrity will increase, as its attractions become known,

From the many flattering notices it has already received, a few of which are at hand, we make several short extracts which may serve to show the growing estimation in which it is held. A large Excursion Party from Ithaca visited it in Aug. 1867. From the account of the trip we take the follow-ing from the Ithaca *Journal* : " This romantic spot has just been opened to visitors and is one of rare beauty. "

The Penn Yan *Express* says, " We think the people of Havana are altogether too modest in their claims as to the beauties and attractions of this Glen. In many respects we think it surpasses the famous Glen at Watkins. Its beautiful cascades, its walled passages, its wierd nooks and caves seem almost indescribable. Nature's handiwork here surpasses the most wonderful works of art." A highly complimentary description of the Glen and vicinity in the Elmira *Gazette,* alludes to " The wonders and striking features of this gem of all Glens." The Watkins *Independent* speaks of its scenery as "Sublime, magnificent—and challenges the admiration of the world."

A correspondent of the Union Springs *Advertiser,* who was at the Masonic Pic-Nic, says, " This Glen is not quite as extensive or as well known as the one at Watkins, but we, as well as all we heard express an opinion, pronounced its scenery in some parts, as finer and more beautiful than anything in the latter." Of Central Gorge, he continues, " it is far ahead of anything of the kind that we have ever seen."

THE GLEN.

McCLURE's GLEN is situated in the town of Montour, near the village of Havana, Schuyler Co., N. Y.

The latter point is accessible several times daily by the trains of the Northern Central Railway, which connect with the Erie at Elmira, and at Canandaigua with the New York Central. Visitors coming by Steamers over Seneca Lake can take the cars at Watkins, three miles from Havana, or may enjoy a pleasant carriage drive of four miles from the Steamboat landing to the entrance of the Glen.

Tourists or parties so desiring, can take the cars at Elmira, Canandaigua, or even Rochester in the morning, and have ample time for a ramble through the Glen and return by the afternoon or evening trains the same day. Those who love to commune with Nature in her most rugged forms, and behold beautiful specimens of elaborate scenery, will perhaps rarely regret a day thus employed.

Supposing the visitor to have arrived at Havana, one of the most important buildings which engage the attention, is THE PEOPLES COLLEGE, situated on a rising eminence in the south-eastern portion of the village. To this Institution is attached a farm of one hundred acres, a portion of which encompasses the mouth of the Glen. Taking either of the streets which lead in the direction of the College, as we proceed southwards up the valley, we leave this edifice at our left. After traveling along the highway for the distance of less than half a mile from the College, our road turns to the left—towards the rising sun. Pursuing this route a short distance, we reach the foot of the hill and also the enclosure or field, at the farther extremity of which the entrance to the Glen is found. To this open plain or plateau might well be given the name of "Do-o-se-o-wah," which signifies in the language of the Iroquois, the aboriginal owners of the soil and perhaps the first admirers of the Glen, a place where the basswoods grow. This plain, surrounded on three sides by tall forest trees, interspersed with shady groves, forms a peculiarly pleasing place, for the assemblage of pleasure or pic-nic parties in summer, and might appear to the attentive observer as a sort of a beautiful foreground to the changing scenes of the picture, constantly presented in the ramble through the Glen to the highlands above.

The first view at the mouth of the ravine or

ENTRANCE OF THE GLEN,

is not an uninteresting one. The action of the waters in centuries past, has gradually worn away the yielding shales on either side of the channel, until they have reached the solid rocks which underlie them. Here the noise of the constantly falling waters breaks upon the ear, while among the adjacent forest trees may be heard the notes of the sweet warbling birds,

> "To approach and behold her varied delights,
> Here with exquisite charms, all Nature invites."

Following the path which leads to Sylvan Bridge just above the first Falls,

THE PORTAL CASCADE,

if we pause for a moment we may behold the foaming waters beneath our feet hastening downwards to the pool at the base of the cascade, where they seem to loiter awhile, e'er continuing their northward bound journey. At this point the waters of McClure's Creek,* in their course from the Highlands, take their final leap into the valley of the Seneca Lake. The stream being a tributary of Catharine Creek, or the Seneca Inlet, the waters of the Glen are borne successively, via. lake and river, to the broad waters of the Atlantic—in their passage sparkling among the Thousand Isles of the St. Lawrence, or rolling sluggishly beneath the heights of Quebec. Here we notice the water-worn and rocky channel which has taken ages for its completion. We may also obtain in passing, a view of the rushing waters leaping from the brink of the Eagle Cliff Falls farther up the ravine. Standing upon the rustic structure, Sylvan Bridge, looking up and down the ravine, we begin to realize many of the hidden beauties of this Section of the Glen—Glen Montour. On the southern bank near the bridge, as well as at points farther up the stream, a singular formation may be seen—a sort of petrified moss. It is called *Calcareous Tufa,* and bears some resemblance to marl.†

Different views of Glen Montour are obtained, according to the route chosen by the visitor in reaching Sylvan Bridge

---

*Named from the first settlers upon its banks. Thomas McClure Sr,. one of the earliest pioneers in this region, came with his family from the valley of Wyoming, along the narrow Indian trail leading from Newtown (now Elmira), to Seneca Lake, about the year 1789. He was a soldier during the dark hours of th Revolution.

†In the Tamarac Swamp where McClure's Creek arises, perhaps six miles eastward, a large bed of marl from which lime is made may be found. The waters fro m the other extremity of this swamp flow into the Chesapeake Bay.

In times of very low water the ascent may be made by crossing the stream just below the Portal Cascade, and clambering up the narrow rocky steps which lead to the tabular rock below the bridge. This affords several fine views which are not observed if the visitor prefers the path on the left, which leads up the stairway, not far from the entrance. The latter structure was not erected until after the close of the first season. The original path, now but rarely used, led through the woods on the south side of the ravine.

Although The Portal Cascade is not over ten or twelve feet in height, still, as the commencement of a long series of varying water-falls, it should not be passed unnoticed, or the chain of miniature falls just above—the Sylvan Rapids. All these seem to foretell the grandeur of the scenery beyond. As we advance through Glen Montour, and obtain a fuller view of

THE EAGLE CLIFF FALLS

in the background, the scene is an impressive one indeed. The proud Eagle Cliffs on either hand tower high above the summit of the Falls. They attract much attention which they assuredly deserve. The one at the right, Prospect Cliff, is one hundred and thirty feet high. The name of this Cascade is derived from the Eyrie, which may be seen attached to the rugged cliff opposite the Falls, where it has been known to exist for a long period of years. in the almost unbroken solitude of Nature. These Falls, the highest in the Glen, taken together with the singular channel just above their brink, form a beautiful picture of glen scenery greatly admired and perhaps rarely equalled. Some protection is here needed to prevent the waters from washing away the table rock near the brink of the cascade, whereby much of its present beauty would be lost. Yonder lofty pine, rearing its head far above the frowning heights, seems almost a standing sentinel. In its top an eagle perched might with sweeping eye command the situation and watch any ill-omened approach to the eyrie below. Although the latter has long been unused by its builders, it is hoped that the airy structure may remain undisturbed. The unbroken fall of the stream at this point is forty-five or fifty feet. Its appearance in the winter of 1867 and '68, was highly interesting. The waters freezing as they fell, the stream became entirely fettered with a solid mass of ice from two to eighteen feet in thickness, so that while the imprisoned waters were unseen, they might be distinctly heard forcing their way through the glittering incrustation.

Ascending the oak stairway and pausing a moment for contemplation, a strange scene is presented. Here, at the commencement of the second sub-division of the Glen— "The Pride of the Senecas"—the stream seems to emerge from a spacious room or hall in the form of an L.

The facings of the rocky sides are so evenly cut or worn by the action of the waters, as to give to this wonderful natural chamber a singularly artistic appearance. The stream here as will be noticed in changing its course, forms a right angle—no less than eight others are also made within a mile from the Portal Cascade. In many places the whitish colored mosses or lichens clinging to the solid walls of this chamber, give it the appearance of having been rudely whitewashed or frescoed. The main hall or passage way is sixty feet in length and about twenty-five in width. The average height of the facings or sides of this natural masonry is perhaps thirty feet. The area of the rocky flooring washed by the waters in the two divisions of this singular chamber—the "Council House of the Senecas"—is over two hundred square yards.

At different stand points in this Section of the Glen, the various views obtained both in ascending and descending are exceedingly beautiful. Much of this romantic beauty consists in the lofty elevation as compared with the spacious amphitheatre in the Glen below, and the novel spectacle of the great artistic skill displayed in the construction of this natural passage—this singular specimen of natural architecture.

The visitor may easily imagine that he beholds pulpits and rostrums in the galleries above—the moss-covered, sloping banks rising far above the bed of the stream, richly laden with the original products of the soil, where, owing to the dense foliage the summer's sun rarely penetrates. Here, in the years that are past have been echoed the wild hunting songs of the Senecas! Here, amid the temples of Nature, the green groves of the wild woods, in the midst of these enchanting scenes of grandeur, they have reverently bowed in allegiance to Hah-wen-ne-yoh, the Great Spirit of the Iroquois!

Following the path which here leads some distance above the bed of the stream, we pass the "Lover's Rest," a small or miniature cave in the rocks merely large enough for two to occupy, which to those romantically inclined might seem a fitting place, to whisper "the old, old story" of

"Two souls with but a single thought,
Two hearts that beat as one."

In one particular, at least, this Glen presents a formidable rival to the preceding one, and that is in the exquisite beauty of

THE CURTAIN CASCADE.

This charming scene is considered by many, as one of the finest views in the Glen. Its beauties, to be appreciated, should be seen from the ledge of rocks on the southern bank of the ravine, several rods below the Cascade. The foaming waters rolling down the shelving rocks, seem to proceed leisurely for a short distance, and then a second abrupt fall is made, after which they sport in the pool below. The lower fall is about eight feet in height and appears as a sort of an apron or curtain. The name, however, is given by the "Curtain Rock "—nearly hidden from observation by the foliage on the left, which completely shuts out from view the upper portion of the Cascade before reaching it, while proceeding along the main path. The height of the two sections, or of the double falls is perhaps thirty-five or forty feet.

One peculiarity of the Glen is worthy of notice. The stream, for perhaps a mile from the entrance of the ravine, makes so many curious changes in its course,—at one moment in a winding or zig-zag direction, then turning perhaps at right angles, that the visitor at times is somewhat bewildered in trying to make out what will come next, or in what direction the pathway will lead to enable him to continue his explorations. This is particularly the case while looking up the ravine, from the point heretofore specified as affording the best view of the Curtain Cascade.

Leaving the latter, let us leisurely proceed along the path crossing over the bridge. A few paces bring us to the base of a short flight of steps, at the summit of which we obtain some fine views. Continuing our progress beneath the frowning cliffs, we again cross the stream and find ourselves upon a narrow ledge of rocks, gazing upon the wild, startling scenery of

CENTRAL GORGE.

This Gorge, as will be inferred from its name, is situated near the center of the Glen. During seasons of great freshets, the angry waters here afford a magnificent spectacle,—madly rushing through the narrow, wierd-like chasm, into the pool below—the "Witches' Caldron." Central Gorge is remarkable for its extent, its grandeur and sublimity. The lover or student of Nature is strikingly impressed with the superior romance and intense wildness of the scene. The same forces which have formed the Glen at one point nearly three hundred feet in width, at another perhaps have reduced its width to three; and the same Power which has caused the lofty cliff to stand out in bold relief, has also caused its base or brow to be adorned with sweetest ferns or wild flowers rare. The scenery here, as viewed from the winding stairways reaching upwards through the narrow Gorge, or from its lofty parapets, is romantic in the extreme, while the Falls o'erhung with bold cliffs almost hidden in the recesses of the ravine, seem to be just what is wanted to complete the picture. From the lower stairway at times the magnificent beauties of the rainbow may be observed, while looking up the Gorge, visible through the snowy veil or mantle of whitened spray arising from the tortuous channel. Looking down the stream after having ascended perhaps two thirds of the upper long stairway, we obtain a fine view of the circular pools far beneath our feet.

Taken together with all its surroundings, Central Gorge is well calculated to inspire the mind with mingled emotions of awe and admiration. Truly, while enraptured in its contemplation or dwelling upon the sublimity of the scene, we are forcibly reminded of the feebleness of human nature, and the thought almost involuntarily arises,—"How manifold are Thy works, in wisdom hast Thou made them all." The beholder seems to stand in one of Nature's wildest haunts. The venerable cliffs, here and there clothed with verdure upon portions of which the golden sunbeams rarely rest; the surging waters hurrying as if in fear from the deep and dark abyss; the variegated mosses fondly clinging to sections of rock which date their creation in buried ages; all these are but a few of the many interesting features here visible. This Gorge varies in depth from fifty to seventy-five or one hundred feet. Before leaving the confines of this remarkable chasm, and while wending our way along its northern escarpment, we find a convenient resting place which comes very opportune to the majority of visitors. Many traverse the Glen in too much haste as far as pleasure or comfort is concerned. But if the visitor has not been too hurried in the ramble thus far, and has taken brief rest occasionally, it will perhaps be ascertained that there are many beautiful and romantic views in the upper sections of the Glen. Certainly several fine cascades, together with many wonderful freaks of Nature, are visible during the remainder of the journey.

Leaving Central Gorge we cross Cavern Bridge, located at the entrance of the Glen of The Caverns. In the latter

we find many strange peculiarities among the narrow, ang-
ling, jagged walls. It might very easily be imagined the resort of a daring Free Booter, situated on some wild and sea
girt shore. A short distance from the bridge on the northern
bank of the stream, may be seen a huge pillar of rock nearly
detached from the main column. It is some twenty-five or
thirty feet in height, and sooner or later this massive stony
structure must fall, as it is operated upon by the frosts of
winter and the rains of summer. The deep cleft or crevice
where the column is severed, in some places is less than a
foot in width. Here and there may be seen openings or fissures
in the various strata, caused by the action of the waters centuries since. Among these singular fissures and caverns in
this interesting locality, one is known as THE INDIAN OVEN.
Near the latter is

THE HERMIT'S CAVE,

situated some eighteen or twenty feet above the bed of the
stream, and is almost entirely concealed from observation.

Its appearance is strikingly romantic from its peculiar location and surroundings. Many by climbing, manage to ex-
plore the cave without artificial assistance. The Indian Oven
is several feet in height and perhaps eight or ten in depth—
much smaller than the Hermit's Cave.

Having now passed through the grandest and wildest portions of the Glen, from this point the Cascades are lessened
in height compared with the larger ones in the lower Glens,
and we shall find less fatigue in climbing. It might here be
remarked, that the upper cascades derive much of their intrin-
sic interest from the marked features or associations distinct-

ively belonging to each. Next, in the order of our progress comes

THE WHISPERING FALLS,

so named from the gentle murmurings of the waters over their rocky bed, as contrasted with the neighboring Cascades.

Near the brink of these Falls a natural table and seat of solid rock may be noticed, and while pausing here in the pleasant summer time viewing the lights and shadows in this portion of the Glen, listening to the songs of the warbling birds together with the rustling of the soft zephyrs breathing through the gently swaying branches, the imagination might easily be prompted to regard this charming locality as the Artist's Retreat or Stubio. While passing along the narrow ledges overhanging the pool at the base of these falls care is needed to keep a firm foothold.

Upon leaving the Whispering Falls, the attentive observer will notice a singular appearance of the ravine, known as Glen Chaos, extending several rods up the stream. The phenomenon—these fallen rocks, now solidly embedded in the ravine—constituting a portion of the flooring along which we traverse, is visible at various points in a variety of shapes, and is faintly traced as far as the Echo Falls. The generally received supposition is, that many centuries ago a great slide occurred here occasioning this confused, chaotic appearance. These prostrate embankments, portions of them thickly coated with heavy and luxuriant mosses, seem evidently to have been ruptured and thrown down by the force of the elements, Some, however, infer that the effect was produced by an earthquake. In some places, the shattered fragments stand up edgewise. A large hemlock, vigorously growing over a section

of these, perhaps far above a hundred years old, is quite a
curiosity.   As we continue our ramble, we approach the Glen
of the Echoes, prominent in which are the

ECHO FALLS.

Before reaching or viewing them, the visitor is agreeably
surprised by the measured sounds of the rumbling waters—
something such as might be heard if the stream was contin-
uously turning the crown-wheel of some flouring mill in the
distance.   To hear them to advantage quiet is necessary, otherwise the attraction or effect of this singular water-fall is
mainly lost or unnoticed.   They are occasioned by the peculiar structure of the Glen and its rocky walls at this point.
The echoes can generally be heard, but depend somewhat upon the condition of the atmosphere, as well as upon the volume of the stream.   While pausing—in the stillness—to hear
the reverberating sounds of welcome wafted through the silent
Glen we are reminded of the following lines, written by the
late song-gifted Bradbury :—

> " Oh, there's music in the waters,
>   Playing on their silver flutes,
> In the autumn night winds sighing
>   Softly over airy lutes."

Similar sounds are heard in the Mammoth Cave, Kentucky.
This Cascade, on account of its strange peculiarity, attracts
much attention.   The action of the waters in the ages that
are past, has resulted in hollowing out one of the deep pools
in which the upper Glens abound.

These Falls afford a curious theme for the imagination to
dwell upon, presenting several questions too great for man to
answer; among them, how many centuries or ages have the

incessant waters been at work in wearing out this spacious pool in the solid rocks, while their unceasing music day by day and night by night has resounded in the rarely broken silence of these romantic wilds? The monotonous sounds have doubtless been made in a greater or less degree, ever since the mammoth landslide or violent convulsion in the Glen below, and perhaps ages before. What must have been the appearance of the locality both before and immediately after this occurrence, and at that time how great must have been the volume of the waters? Did they then reach the ocean by their present course, or were they mingled with the broad waters of the Susquehanna? Or did they take some other— perhaps an opposite route?

Climbing up over the rocks perhaps twelve feet in height on the north side of the Cascade of the Echoes, we enter an interesting locality, known as the Glen of the Pools. Many of the basins or wells found here are exceedingly beautiful, varying greatly in size and shape. Conspicuous among them are the two circular ones, a short distance above the Echo Falls—the Rival Pools. While looking down into one of these through the clear bright water, a striking resemblance carved in the solid rock, to the head of some huge animal is discovered—an uncommon specimen of natural sculpture.

The next point of interest is

THE FAIRIES' CASCADE.

. At its base is found another of those beautiful pools— the deepest in the Glen. The charms of this unpretending Cascade are enhanced by the stillness, and by the beauty of its situation and surroundings. Not far above it there are several small, singularly shaped pools. One resembles a helmet, another an artist's pallet. The many varieties of mosses which are seen in nearly all sections of the Glen, but especially in the " Forest Grotto" near this cascade, are much admired and viewed in connection with the numerous plants, shrubs or flowers every where visible, present interesting subjects to those who love botanical studies. From the Fairies' Cascade, our pathway leads along the northern bank of the ravine. Soon, we catch a glimpse in the distance of

THE SUMMIT FALLS.

Aside from other considerations, these Falls are possessed of no slight interest, from the fact that two singular formations are found in the rocky bed of the stream near their brink. They are familiarly known as " *The Petrified Hats.*" They are certainly worthy the inspection of the curious, and contain a pleasant study to the geologist. As many visit the Glen without seeing them, it may not be amiss to locate or describe them more particularly. They bear an almost perfect resemblance in shape and appearance to two gentlemens' hats, as if sunken or compressed in the bed of the rock, are always and completely submerged by the water. The reader will find a humorous poetic allusion to them in another por. tion of this work.

And now having passed through the Glen, the visitor in retracing his steps will perhaps find occasionally some attractive view, which escaped his observation in ascending. But, whether the visitor decides to return to the valley through the Glen or not, he may be amply repaid perhaps, if the ramble be continued over the table lands, so as to include the magnificent view of

SENECA LAKE FROM THE HIGHLANDS

of the Glen, which forms one of the many delightful land-scapes in which Western New York abounds. Viewed in summer or autumn, the valley and hillsides, with the lovely Seneca in the distance, present a varied panorama of exceeding loveliness—

> "Most beautiful lake? thou art ever the same,
> As when Seneca braves to thee gave their name."

This lake in some respects is remarkable. It is vastly deeper than any of the inland lakes of the State—is thirty feet deeper than Lake Ontario, and more than double the depth of Lake Erie. Its waters have been several times partially, but never entirely frozen over, since the first white settlements were made in this region. As the lake is separated from the Glen by a distance of only four miles, many of the charms of the latter are enhanced by the proximity of the former.

Standing upon these table lands, we find that the space of the few intervening furlongs "lends enchantment to the view," and although town lines may come between, yet the surprised beholder emerging from the Glen, who first views the lake from this altitude—perhaps four hundred feet above its surface—forgets for the moment all save the contemplation of the romantic scene. Prof. Towler of Hobart College, Geneva, not inappropriately classes this Glen, among the "beauties of Seneca Lake."

At this point of our progress, let us read a few paragraphs from the pen of a talented writer, Chas. Hazard, Esq., upon his return from a visit to the Glen and its surroundings. After describing the former he says:

"Reader you can make it complete yourself—study it up at your leisure by going to McClure's Glen, and you will be all the better for it. We, ourselves, will come out from among these grand beauties by way of the hill. Standing on the mountain's summit what a beautiful panorama is spread before us of the outer world. God never smiled on a lovelier valley than this. Look away to the North: See stretching beyond, as far as the eye can reach, bewitching Seneca sleeps in the afternoon sun—fair as a maiden in summer *siesta*. The declining rays of the long afternoon clothe her bosom with gossamer wrappings of gold—as if to hide her pearly charms from the gaze of men—while across the swarthier bosom of Mother earth the same yellow-hued bands are flung."

The surrounding country thickly dotted with thrifty farmhouses and cultivated fields, affords a delightful prospect contrasted with the picturesque villages which adorn the valley below. Steamers gracefully float on the lake, where less than a century since the canoes and bateaux of the Senecas were seen. Heavily laden trains course through the smiling valley, which less than a century since contained a solitary Indian settlement, surrounded by the corn-fields and apple-orchards* of Queen Catharine. Along the shores of yonder lake which

"Bright reflects the polar star,"

have been heard the war-songs of the Iroquois, where also they have wonderingly listened to the teachings of the early French and English Missionaries of the cross. There a Kirkland, "traveling upon snow-shoes, and camping at night upon and under hemlock boughs," in his journey to the Sen-

---

*Few are the remnants of these orchards remaining in the vicinity, dearly prized by the red men, planted and tended with care near the graves of their ancestors, or beneath whose shade the conquering hosts of Sullivan were encamped, on their way to the more remote settlements of the Senecas and Cayugas.

ecas' Lake in 1765—one of the first Protestant Missionaries in Western New York—has endeavored to benefit the unlettered Senecas or "The Great Hill People."* Upon its shores, also, the latter have given marked attention to the lengthy perorations of *Jemima Wilkinson,* " A Preacheress of the Eighteenth Century," or as she was styled by herself and followers, " The Universal Friend." The first residence of the latter, was upon the western bank of the lake—near the present village of Dresden, where she arrived with her retinue in 1789. Some of her adherents had preceded her a year or two in search of some "fertile unsettled region far from towns and cities where the " Universal Friend" and her followers, might live undisturbed in peace and plenty in the enjoyment of their peculiar religion." Concerning her coming to the Seneca Lake Region, the following may be found in Turner's History:

"William Hencher, the Pioneer at the mouth of the Genesee River, then lived at Newtown Point, and helped her on with his teams through the woods to Catharinestown (Havana). His surviving son, who accompanied the expedition, well remembers "The Friend," her singular dress and singularity as it seemed to him, of a woman controlling and directing men in all things appertaining to the journey. It seemed to him a " one woman power, "if the form of expres-

---

& In Seaver's Life of Mary Jemison, otherwise called The White Woman, we find; "the tradition of the Seneca Indians in regard to their origin is, that they broke out of the earth from a large mountain at the head of Canandaigua Lake, and that mountain they still venerate as the place of their birth; thence they derive their name " Ge-nun-de-wah," or Great Hill, and are called "The Great Hill People,"which is the true definition of the word Seneca.
   The great hill at the head of Canandaigua lake, from whence they sprung, is called Genundewah, and has for a long time past been the place where the Indians of that nation have met in council, to hold great talks, and to offer up prayers th the Great Spirit, on account of its having been their birth place. *
   * * * To this day(1842) the Indians visit that sacred place to mourn the loss of their friends, and to celebrate some rites that are peculiar to themselves.- To the knowledge of white people there has been no timber on the great hill, since it was first discovered by them, though it lay apparently in a state of nature for a great number of years, without cultivation."

sion may be changed with the sex; yet he gratefully remembers her kindness and hospitality when his father's family came through the wilderness, and stopped at her residence, on their way to the Genesee River."

According to Mr Turner, one of the prominent early settlers of Yates Co., "insists that the old story of her promising to 'walk on the water' is wholly false". An informant of the writer, also residing in Schuyler Co., but in his younger days a frequent attendant upon Jemima's exhortations, says that many falsehoods were published or circulated concerning her.

But, whatever the character of this singular woman, many anecdotes, whether true or untrue, have been rehearsed far beyond the limits of the Seneca Lake Region, and the influence or tendencies of her peculiar doctrines, as taught in the wilds of Western New York; either at her residence* to the the backwoods pioneers, or to the wondering Senecas on the shores of their beautiful lake have not as yet, perhaps, entirely lost their force. It is a little singular, also, that within the county of Ontario as then organized, which included her residence, "The New Jerusalem,"† or the "promised land," as she termed it, Mormonism and Modern Spiritualism have since originated.

Although during the Revolution no battles were fought

---

*The first framed house in Western New York. The gristmill, built by her followers, on the outlet of Keuka (Crooked) Lake, was, also, the first erected within the same limits.

†Shortly after her primary location was made, two of her followers purchased an original township, in Yates County for 1s. 3d. per acre, Jemima immediately gave it the name of Jerusalem which it still retains. Of this purchase a farm of one thousand acres was set apart for the use of Jemima and her more immediate household. The large dwelling in which her meetings were held and in which she resided at the time of her death—in 1819—is still standing, situated a few miles from Branch Port. From the strange history of this singular woman, even to the house itself, no slight interest attaches. A portion of the time during the late war it was used as a Soldiers' Home.

upon the Seneca, still the cannonading of Sullivan's Army was heard reverberating on the shores, above the "Painted Rocks," or among the shales at Big Stream Point and Lodi, bringing terror and desolation to the Indian Settlements in the vicinity of the lake, especially at Catharinestown, Peach Orchard, Apple Town and Canadesaga (now Geneva). Consequently items of interest concerning the lake will generally partake of a more peaceful nature. In the early settlement of the region, and since, its waves, however, have occasionally assisted in terminating various engagements. In this view, perhaps, the following pleasant reminiscence of this romantic lake may not here be inappropriate. The first celebration of the marriage ceremony among the pioneers of Ovid, Seneca Co., was quite interesting. All of the particulars are not at hand; whether the golden morn, or the silvery moonlight furnished the hour; whether the joyful party proceeded to Catharinestown or Canadesaga*, for the present writing is immaterial. One thing was certain, the waves of the Seneca sparkled between the bridal party and the nearest justice authorized to perform the ceremony. No "Langdon" or "Magee" was in readiness to bear them to their destination. Viewed in any light, however, the excursion upon such an errand could have been regarded only as a pleasant undertaking. It is sometimes an embarassing duty for a backwoods justice to unite one couple in marriage, but what must have been the surprise of the one in question, when he beheld not one, but *three* couples—fair daughters and hardy

*The latter, perhaps, as at about that time—1793—it is related that a smaller party at Catharinestown visited Tioga Point (now Athens) on horseback, upon a similar errand.

sons* of Seneca, approaching his residence, as was the case upon this occasion.

In the year 1792, three hundred years after the discovery of America, a traveler in describing the country between Albany and Niagara, wrote: "Twelve miles west of Cayuga I struck the Canadasaga (Seneca) Lake—no inhabitant upon this road.† This lake is the handsomest piece of water I ever beheld."

Since that time, evidences have not been wanting, that the opinion of this traveler was not formed without foundation. While speculating upon the future condition of the country through which he passed, he introduced the following singularly prophetic quotation:

"Here happy millions their own lands possess,
No tyrant awes them, nor no lords oppress."

Later, in 1820, a writer incog—Hibernicus—whose letters were afterwards published in book form, writes from Geneva: "I like the air and scenery of this place so much that I cannot leave it without regret. The spacious hotel is replete with accommodations. The village hangs over the pellucid lake, which stretches like a mighty river towards the south, and the eye is lost in tracing its extent."

---

*While this work was in press, one of these, Mr. Abraham A. Covert, nearly one hundred years of age, a highly respected citizen of Ovid, and one of its earliest pioneers, was called away from the scene of his earthly labors. The following is taken from the obituary notice published in the Ovid *Bee*, at the time of his death: "Mr. Covert was a most exemplary and excellent man in all the relations of life. It has often been remarked of him that 'he had not an enemy in the world,' nor has any one ever been heard to say aught against him." With the history of the remaining bridegrooms, the writer is not familiar, their names however were Joseph Wilson and Enoch Stewart.

†This traveler could not have taken the route of the old "Seneca Turnpike," afterwards "The State Road," as settlements were then already commenced at Seneca Falls and Waterloo—at the former place by one who had shared the trials of White Plains and Valley Forge, and who afterwards had served under the banners of Sullivan.

. In another letter dated at Ithaca, he says: "The scenery of these lakes is alternately picturesque, beautiful and sublime. Before the revolution of a century, this country will become consecrated to classic inspiration, 'live in description, and grow green in song.'" Although in another letter he remarks: "I have seen bells no where but at the great inn at Geneva, and scrapers no where but at the sign of the whale in Chitteningo," still these accommodations, together with almost untold other ones, have long since been supplied throughout what was then denominated as the "Western Region," while developments of the "West" have extended over thousands of square miles and millions of acres, rich in resources, towards the setting sun.

As an item of local interest, it might be remarked that the first sloop launched upon the Seneca Lake, was the "Seneca," built under the auspices of Col. Charles Williamson, in 1796, to ply between Geneva and Catharinestown, sailing up the Inlet from the head of the lake. Of the people convened from all quarters to witness the launch of this vessel, it is recorded that "natives of every State in the Union, and of every nation of Europe, were to be found in the assemblage." (Doc. Hist. N. Y., Vol. 2.) Of the steamers* which in later years have navigated the lake, the first was "the Seneca Chief," Capt. Robert Romney. Her first through trip was made July 4, 1828, an occasion of much rejoicing. This boat, built by Seth Huntley, for the Romney Bros., at a later

*Of these steamers generally, the writer would mention that it appears to have been a time-honored observance carefully handed down upon this lake, that each succeeding vessel on leaving the stocks should always contain among other indispensable requisites, a well furnished and abundant larder. Owing to this, the atmosphere of the lake or some other undefined cause, travelers usually upon these boats are rarely at a loss for an appetite—never for the means of satisfying the same.

date was remodeled and her name changed to "Geneva."
She never survived her twentieth anniversary, being destroyed by fire, July 4, 1848. In those days, furnishing "steamboat wood" was a matter of no little importance along the
lake; but long since, the "hand barrows" so common upon
the decks of the "Canadesaga" or "Richard Stevens" have
disappeared from their successors. The fireman who pa-
tiently attends to his constant duties in the hold, whether in
December or July, is no longer annoyed with sections of
blackened pines from a burned "summer fallow," or the
splinters of the hemlock, for with the changes of time, the
Fall Brook coal regions of Pennsylvania furnish a funda-
mental means of propelling the steamers, which at present
are the "Elmira," "Magee," "Arnot," "Field," and "Langdon." Besides these, there are several smaller craft, tugs,
yachts, etc. The first vessel which reached New York City
from Seneca Lake, was the "Mary and Hannah," of Hector
Falls, named from the wives of her owners. Upon reaching
her destination, she attracted no little attention, and was
presented with a set of sails and colors.

A PIONEER OF THE VALLEY.

" But our undaunted pioneers
    Have conquests more enduring won,
  In scattering the night of years
    And opening forests to the sun.

＊　　＊　　＊　　＊　　＊

  The storms they met with bosoms bared,
    And bloodless triumphs bought by toil;
' The wild beast from his cavern scared,
    And clothed in bloom the virgin soil."—Hosmer.

One of the first known white navigators who traversed either Seneca or Cayuga Lakes was Mr. George Mills—in 1788, one of the earliest pioneers at Havana.

At the age of fourteen he had served six months in the Revolution, "three for his father and three for himself." He came to the Seneca Lake valley from Pennsylvania in company with Mr. John Richardson. Remaining some time at Catharinestown, when but two families resided here, they proceeded to Cayuga County, where Mr. Mills was the first white man who held a plow. In his later years, while speaking of this, he described it as sport to see the natives—the Senecas and Cayugas—watch the motions of the plow as it bounded out of the ground when caught in the roots of the stumps or trees, expressing their admiration by tossing up sods and dirt in the air. After residing two years in Cayuga, Mr. Mills returned to Catharinestown, locating upon a portion of the L'Hommedieu Patent,* on the eastern bank of Catharine Creek. Here in his humble cabin of logs, in 1797, he entertained Louis Phillippe, then the Duke of Orleans. In his Indian batteaux he navigated the waters of the Seneca long before a sloop, schooner, or perhaps even a periauger, had rested upon its surface, to say nothing of the commodious steamers which may now be daily seen plowing

---

* A tract of 4000 acres, located by Hon. Ezra l'Hommedieu, of Southold, Suffolk Co., N. Y., one of the first in the vicinity of Havana. This patent embraced portions of the present villages of Havana and Watkins; the Sulphur Spring on l'Hommedieu Creek and Aunt Sarah's Falls at the former place, the entrance of the Watkins Glen; and a locality known as "Rock Cabin" on the opposite side of the valley, were included within its limits. Its Long Island purchaser, for years a State Senator, was one of the principal originators of the movement culminating in the appointment of The Regents of the University. The solitary elm upon the beach of the Lake, one of the "monuments" in the original survey, near the extensive Coal Transhipment Works of the late Hon. John Magee of Watkins, is still standing. This venerable tree for many years shaded portions of three counties—Chemung, Tompkins and Steuben.

its limpid waters. For years his location, " Mills' Landing," and prior to the extension of the Erie Canal west of Monte-zuma, was the head of inland canal or river navigation. As the population grew in numbers, the tonnage of his vessels was increased. With the latter he carried on quite an exten-sive commerce between the "West" and the East—"Mills' Landing" (Havana) and Schenectady, via. the "Wood Creek" route. At the time of the present writing, April, 1868, the warehouse built and occupied by Mr. M., previous to the extension of the Seneca Inlet navigation, is still standing, falling into disuse for forwarding purposes after the comple-tion of the Chemung Canal. This enterprising and hardy pioneer was the first Post Master in this region. The receipts of the first quarter were thirty-seven and one-half cents, of which the general government received one-half.

In the columns of the Havana *Journal* at the time of the death of Father Mills, as he was familiarly called, in Dec. 1858, it is recorded that " he was one of the oldest Free Masons in the State, having become a member of that fraternity in 1800 ; and from the same paper we quote from the resolutions passed by Chemung (now Myrtle) Lodge at Havana, " a bright Star from the Constellation of our cher-ished Order has fallen, a Pillar in the Arch of our Temple is broken, and a Burning Taper in front of our Altar has been . extinguished." His funeral was attended with Masonic, Mil-itary and civic honors.

On the western side of the valley at our feet, near the Montour Cemetery, may be seen

THE HAVANA FALLS.

During seasons of high water, when a rushing torrent

madly dashes from their heights, the scene is magnificently grand. At other times the waters are temporarily diverted from their natural channel for manufacturing purposes.

In the MSS. of the late Hon. Thomas Maxwell, of Elmira, N. Y., the Indian name of these Falls has been preserved, as will be seen by the following extract. Space forbids copying it entire, as well as other interesting matters pertinent to this locality, which may be found in Cheney's "Historical Sketch of the Chemung Valley, etc.," published in the Havana *Journal* in 1867.

"In a conversation held with Red Jacket, at Bath, in 1828, he informed me that when a child he was present at a great council-fire of the tribes at Shenandoah, in Virginia. The various nations were represented by their most distinguished orators, but the greatest among them was Logan, a Cayuga, who had removed from his residence on the Cayuga to Shemokin, on the Susquehanna. Red Jacket remarked that he was so highly delighted with Logan's eloquence, that he resolved to devote himself to public speaking, and to follow Logan as his model. He said that he was in the habit of speaking in the woods where he could find a water-fall, where he exercised his voice amid the roaring waters, to acquire the necessary command and tone to address large assemblies. One of his favorite resorts for this purpose, was the magnificent water-fall at Havana. The name of the stream was She-qua-gah, or as he interpreted it, "the place of the roaring waters." The water-fall seems to have been his peculiar inspiration. In early life the beautiful She-qua-gah, and in his mature years the mighty Ne-au-gua-rah, (I give his own pronunciation,) were his favorite haunts."

This celebrated Seneca chieftain was born in 1750, near Canoga, Seneca county, N, Y. The following is from one of his speeches in 1827 :

"It grieves my heart, when I look around and see the situation of my people—once united and powerful, now weak and divided. I feel sorry for my nation; when I am gone to the other world, when the Great Spirit calls me away, who among my people can take my place? Many long years have I guided the nation. * * * The Lord gave his red children their lands: General Washington said they were sure, * * * as long as I can stand in my moccasins I will do all I can for my nation."

Conspicuous among other commodious structures which adorn the village of Havana, as seen from these Highlands, is the MONTOUR HOUSE, a spacious Hotel erected some years since, where ample arrangements are made for the comfort and convenience of the traveler or tourist sojourning in the locality. Yonder stands

THE PEOPLES COLLEGE,

a stately edifice designed to minister popular education to the public. It was chartered in 1853, and its chief patron for some years was the late Hon. Charles Cook.

The Institution is now conducted under Masonic auspices, in connection with an Asylum for the benefit of Masonic orphans. In aid of this enterprise a Festival and Pic-Nic was held at Jones' Wood, New York, Sept. 11th, 1867. In the Masonic Ode by William Ross Wallace, written for this occasion and delivered by him, we find the following flattering mention:

"Never shone for a location grander scenery, richer sod,
All imparadised by the blessing of the Orphan's Father—GOD."

Ever since the College was first located at Havana, no small degree of interest in its ultimate completion and success has been cherished, not only in this immediate vicinity, but more or less throughout the Empire State, as well as other States of the Union.

In regard to this enterprise, we quote from the editorial columns of a late number of the *National Examiner*, of New York City, the following;

"As will be seen by a reference to the proceedings of the Grand Lodge, that M. W. Grand Body has recognized and approved the efforts that have been made by the bretheren who have labored so faithfully in the good cause, and further, have recomended the School and Asylum to the Lodges and Fraternity throughout the State. New life will be infused into the movement by this action; many who have been hesitating with a natural fear that the charity was an unauthorized one, will now come foward and bend their best energies to the work, and when at the next annual communication of the Grand Lodge the Trustees report, as instructed, the amount of funds collected and expended, we feel sure that the Fraternity of Free and Accepted Masons throughout the State of New York will feel proud of the Institution that they have taken under their protection."

In the same paper, also, we notice that the Second Annual Grand Pic-Nic, in aid of the Masonic School and Asylum at Havana, is to be held at Jones' Woods, on Tuesday July 7th, 1868.

CATHARINESTOWN.*

In the valley a short distance from the entrance of the Glen, and near the site of the present village of Havana, was the residence of Queen Catharine Montour, of the Senecas. The Indian village Catharinestown—her former home—was destroyed in 1779, during Sullivan's campaign. Slight traces through the valley still exist, along which a portion of the Revolutionary army—Sullivan's command numbering

---

*The present township of Catharine, Schuyler County—named from Queen Catharine Montour— was formed in 1798, as *Catharines*, from Newtown, then in the County of Tioga. From the original territory of Catharines the towns of Veteran and Catlin in Chemung, Dix and Montour in Schuyler Counties, have since been taken.

five thousand men—marched through the dense wilderness into the heart of the Indian country—the Long House of the Iroquois.* This road, once an Indian trail from the Susquehanna to the lakes, passed between the Glen and the College, across the College farm, extending northward on the eastern side of the valley between the twin lakes—the Seneca and the Cayuga. Probably in order to intimidate the Indians, after leaving the Chemung river Sullivan's force was extended or drawn out six miles in their line of march, and cannon were fired at nightfall to herald the onward progress of the troops.

The campaign was a short and decisive one, and from its results the Iroquois, or Six Nations of New York Indians, never recovered.

It is interesting at this day, however, to reflect that after the close of the Revolution, it was the earnest desire of Washington, who had planned and sent out expeditions against them, that a conciliatory policy should be extended to the Six Nations, and that a veil might be drawn over their conduct. In the furtherance of a similar design, several Reservations in the Empire State were granted to them by Government, which are yet peopled by their descendants.— Some of these—particularly of the Senecas—enlisted during the late unhappy strife to preserve our National unity.

One of them, Col. Ely S. Parker, is at present on the staff of that General who received the first intelligence of the surrender of a long, protracted and hopeless struggle—"the lost cause"—which position he has occupied for several years.

---

†The Iroquois originally consisted of five Nations, but was increased to six by the adoption of the Tuscaroras. The latter event was commemorated by hanging up a cradle in the General Council House.

The generally received supposition concerning Queen Catharine Montour is, that she was a daughter of an early French Governor of Canada, taken captive when a child, afterwards becoming the wife of a Seneca Chief. She held a prominent place in the estimation of her people, occasionally attending various councils at Albany, Philadelphia, and other places. After Sullivan's campaign, she resided for some time near Niagara.

At an early day in the history of Western New York, Catharinestown was a locality of no small importance. For many years, it, afterwards called "Catharine's Landing," or "Mills' Landing," and previous to the building of the Erie Canal, was the head of western inland navigation. The writer having been courteously permitted access to advance sheets of the " Historical Sketch of Elmira and the Chemung Valley," in Gallatian's City Directory of Elmira for 1868, published by Messrs. Wheeler and Watts of the same place, an extract is given as pertinent to the subject. From the portion of it refering to the changes in the boundaries or limits of the old county of Tioga, in connection with later developments, we select ;

" In the minds of the surviving pioneers and their descendants, however, no modern lines of demarkation can separate their pioneer fame, nor obliterate cherished memorials or ancient landmarks upon the page of truthful history.   *   *   *   *   *

From the date of the first infant effort at internal improvement, commencing with the issue of the first commission in 1797, to Phineas Catlin and Matthew Carpenter, (the latter of whom was succeeded by John Hendy,) " to lay out the road leading from Catskill Landing, upon the Hudson, to Catharinestown, in the county of Tioga," to the projection and completion of the New York and Erie

Rail Road, through "the Southern Tier," *   *   *   the pioneer struggles and patriotic efforts of their inhabitants have been encouraged and strengthened by a sympathetic and heartfelt mutuality. Their hopes and fears have been in unison; their defeats and victories shared in the kindest brotherhood—co-equals in public spirit, and in its substantial and enduring rewards."

Those who would seek more particularly, to locate the site of the ancient village of Catharinestown, are refered to the fact, that upon the decease of a prominent citizen of Havana, when the autumnal leaves were falling in 1866, who for many years had ardently labored for its prosperity and advaancement, his final resting place was chosen in accordance with a written request, found after his decease, that he might be buried near "the Queen Catharine mound." In fulfilling this request, with other accompanying instructions, a portion of his possessions were set apart for burial purposes, as indicated where to-day he rests after a long and active life.

The visitor who appraoches his silent grave, will notice, that from it may be seen many cherished enterprises—some uncompleted, perhaps—in which the heart now stilled forever, was so long and deeply interested.

Concerning this spot, we subjoin the following from the editorial columns of the Elmira *Gazette*, a continuation of the extract previously given. (See page 32.)   •

"Turning from the Lake's enchanting beauty, to the valley's rivaling splendor of fertility, our eyes fall on a lonely grave opposite to us in the valley below—THE GRAVE OF CHARLES COOK. He who called into being so much of the cultured wealth and busy enterprise of that thriving village, sleeps there—the long last sleep, whence none may awake. A rough wooden fence encloses the grave

—no monument as yet emblazens his worth. Tis well if it were never changed from what it is now—common, crusty worded, (but mellow hearted,) CHARLES COOK, wants no better monument than what Havana is. Let her people remember him ever."

Reader, the more descriptive part of our little volume is nearly completed. Should you ever visit the Glen, you will find much to examine and admire, of which no mention is made in these pages. And after you have explored its heretofore hidden mysteries, remember that other delightful glens and cascades abound in the locality. They are well worthy of an inspection.

Among other points of attraction in this valley, a short distance south of the Glen is a charming Cascade*—Sullivan's Falls. It was visited in 1779 by the officers of Sullivan's expedition, and is mentioned in the records of that campaign. Some of its features are essentially different from any of the neighboring cascades.

Prominent among the Glens in this vicinity is the one at Watkins,† which has already obtained a wide notoriety, and is annually visited by thousands. The banks of the beautiful Seneca are also adorned with several fine cascades, and abound in picturesque scenery. Among these waterfalls and which may be seen from the decks of the steamers, may be mentioned particularly those at Hector Falls, Rock Stream, Big Stream and Lodi. At certain seasons of the year, and

*Near the residence of T. Appoleon Cheney, LL.D., a well-known writer, who has made many valuable researches and reports respecting the early history and antiquities of Western New York.

†An interesting Hand Book for the use of Tourists visiting the Glen at Watkins, by George M. Ellwood, Esq., contains much that is serviceable to its visitors.

especially during heavy freshets, they present magnificent views.

The glens and cascades near the head of Seneca Lake, in some respects have a united or common interest, no two of them being alike, each adds to the attraction of the others. Taken together, they form a circle of natural beauties that are seldom surpassed.

Less than a day's pleasant drive from the Glen at Havana, brings the visitor to Enfield Falls, or to the Falls of Taughannock, near Goodwin's Point on Cayuga Lake,* celebrated r their great height and the picturesque embellishments of their rural surroundings.

Besides other summer resorts, Cayuta Lake, a small sheet of water in the town of Catharine, a few miles from Havana, is much visited by pic-nic and fishing parties. It is pleasantly situated, and is rapidly growing into public favor.

In Schuyler County, also, two other small lakes may be found near its western borders, in the town of Tyrone, which afford varied attractions to the visitor. These three coquetish minor lakes, from their situation, flow into the Susquehanna River; while the majority of the larger lakes in the State are tributary to the St. Lawrence.

Not far from Little Lake, in Tyrone, is the famous Crystal Spring,† in Barrington, Yates Co., which attracts many visitors.

---

*The village of Ithaca at the head of this lake is also much noted for its enchanting, varied, and beautiful scenery.

† This spring or fountain in which nature and art in one sense might both be considered as stockholders, was discovered while sinking a well during the oil excitement a few years since. At the depth of forty three feet the waters burst forth from their subterranean caverns, and have since continued uninterruptedly to flow; for them valuable medicinal qualities are claimed. The nearest Rail Road Station to Crystal Spring is at Starkey.

Descriptive Poems.

McCLURE'S GLEN.
[1857.]

BY JOHN B. LOOK.

How wild the scene! How wond'rous wild!
Here Nature lived when but an infant child,
And here her leisure hours devoted all
To play strange freaks with this terrestrial ball:
One hour she lifted rock on rock most high,
Another, planned a flower to please the eye;—
A mason quite, and yet a painter good:
She piled the rocks o'er which to leap the flood,
And then these flowers, with richly painted hue,
(None lovelier graced a bank or richer grew,)
All, all were touched with that Inventive hand,
As if this art was at its sole command.
This moss on which we rest,—oh, beauteous green—
A carpet quite;—none richer e'er was seen;—
These trees! ah, how they shield us from the rays
Of burning heat that come in burning days.
'Tis all complete:—the brooklet, rock and bow'r,
The carpet green, the shrub and scented flow'r,
All, all commingle in this grandeur wild,—
By Nature reared when Nature was a child.

   *   *   *   *

We'll rest us here; and now behold the scene:
The rocks are rough and dark the deep ravine;

4

The sunlight lingers never where we tread,
And cheering rays ne'er find a welcome bed;
But lo, we hear the water's awful fall,
And feel the spray hie up the dampened wall;
Here, at "high twelve" the wand'rer finds it night,
And, though the sky is clear and heaven is bright,
He dwells amid a never ending storm,
Without one beam his chilly limbs to warm;
He sees the drops that leap from yonder hight,
And in the darkness deems them orbs of light;
But scarce they live ere they are doomed to die,
And coldly pass us as they onward fly.
How much like time, how much like man they are:
A moment here, then gone, we know not where.
But so it is with time, with men, with all
The fleeting things on this terrestrial ball;
A moment given, as quick as thought 'tis fled,—
To day we live, to-morrow will be dead;
To day we're happy with the blessings given,
To-morrow 'll find us in the courts of Heaven.

'Tis change man loves, and Nature placed it here:
Just look below and see the sunlight clear;
A rainbow now doth overhang the vault,
Where quick the rushing waters make a halt.
Ah, " bow of promise," welcome to our sight,
Thrice welcome, rainbow, to our new-born light;—
Too long we tarried in that drear abode,
Where shadows die along the watery road.
Where every crackling bush doth thrill the heart,
And day and night ne'er meet and never part.
Good night, then darkness, and warm welcome day,
With varied bow, caused by the leaping spray;
Here once again we find the wild-flower's bed:
Fresh blooming roses, with their petals spread,

The blue *Viola* nestle as they're prest,
And woodland-songsters sing the gods to rest,
While ev'ry drop looks like a world on fire,
Hung up in space for man alone t' admire.
Ah, ROBERT BURNS, you'd written not of Doon,
Had you here reveled in the month of June,
Had you perchance, this lovely dell espied,
With HIGHLAND MARY by your throbbing side,
The banks of Doon would ne'er have raised your pen,
'Til you'd exhausted this—McCLURE'S GLEN.

But here we are, now at our journey's end,
These awful crags no mortal can descend;
The waters plunge some hundred feet, or more,
And frothy madness hugs the rock-bound shore;
The trees around are drench'd as in a show'r,
So leaps the misty liquid up the tow'r;
So long the rocks have wept, perhaps in fear,
That all are furrowed with a brineless tear,
'Til every flower, in imitation true,
Has learned to weep an innocent adieu.
No longer gaze, our hearts with sadness fill;—
Let's trace our winding course up yonder hill;
Let's mount the brow with steady step and firm,
For day's declining, night will soon return;
And who would tarry mid these awful wilds,
Where howling waters echo forth for miles,
And hear sweet daylight, dying in the west,
Proclaiming, man, here take your nightly rest!
Then, as we'd hasten from the owls and bats,
We'll rest us not 'till safe on yonder flats,
And there, at evening, view the last grand leap,
Of tired waters o'er the rock bound steep.

The watery moon, with face half hid from view
And beams just dampened with the falling dew,

Now smiling, looked o'er hilltops far away,
As if to see how Sol had spent the day,.
Then o'er the mead she kindly threw a sheen,
And dropped the mountain veil that hung between,
And in full glory gazed upon our earth,—
A full-grown moon, that seem'd full grown at birth.
Now sit we on a flow'r-deck'd, moss-grown, knoll,
And view the trembling waters, as they roll
From off a plane inclined, with rapid force,
As if before they'd traveled o'er the course
And motion wished, to leap from yonder brow,
Where stars are mirrored and are tumbling now.
You've leaped your last, the hazard race is o'er,
The Glen's behind, the pebbly brook before;
Here moon-kiss'd rosebuds bend them o'er your breast,
And new-born zephyrs fan you into rest.

—Our thoughts run backward as the moon runs high.
We lose these scenes for those long since gone by:
Young Indians here were wont to skip and play,
And court their lovers at the death of day;
When all was quiet, save the wigwam smoke,
And mighty forests felt no white man's stroke,
Young red men rambled in this lone retreat,
And whispered love in native accents sweet;
Here native lips have pressed on native brows;
Here love exchanged her simple, earnest vows;
Here the " Great Spirit," through their noble " Chief,"
Hath bound the Squaw and Indian in one sheaf;
Here death hath been, and yet we see no stones
To mark the resting of their ancient bones;
A nation slept within this loved abode,
Ere white man's axe had marked the traveled road;—
Here once a village, of no small renown,
An'Indian village,—lovely wigwam town,

Was seen by men who sought to kill their "Braves,"
And drive the weak from Seneca's blue waves;
Here, too, Queen CATHARINE bore a noble part,—
She loved the red man as she loved her heart,—
MONTOUR her name, a name forever dear
To those familiar with her bold career.
But, hold! on yonder mound we mark a trace
Of some who tarried with this exiled race;
Some kindly hand hath reared a marble white,
That yonder glistens in the moon-beams bright.

Sleep on, sleep on; oh, red man, soundly sleep;
For should you wake, 'twould only be to weep;
The place you'd know not—Brothers all are gone,—
They lingered, sighed, and left us one by one.
The iron horse—you know not what I mean—
A thing of life now flies the hills between;
The merry boatmen sing their midnight song,
On the broad "ditch" that lies your grave along.
A little way, HAVANA rears its head,
Where fifteen hundred white men daily tread;
From here we gaze, and lo, yon lofty spire,
In moon-beams, looks like monument on fire;
A thousand lights in thousand dwellings burn,—
You'd call them wigwams,—that's the Indian term;—
The mills are sounding—what know you of Mills?
Nought save one GEORGE, who lives just o'er the hills;
A man of ninety, ninety two, or more,
Who oft has told us tales of days of yore;
You scarce would know him, Indian, should you rise,
The "Master" soon will call him to the skies;
Old age has robbed him of his youthful bloom,
And soon, like you, he'll sleep within the tomb.
But, we must leave you—no, we'll not go yet,—
We've lingered long, our locks are getting wet;

But ere we go, there's one thing more we'll tell:
Soon on yon rise you'll hear a *College bell*;
The "PEOPLE'S COLLEGE" there will lift its dome,
Where books and labor 'll find an equal home.

Now, fare-thee-well; sleep on, and take thy rest,—
We'll to our home—'tis poor, but there we're blest,—
And as we go we'll mind us of your race,
By seeing CATHARINE's name in sightly place,—
CHARLES COOK has reared a monument—'tis well,—
Its name "MONTOUR."—now Indian, fare-thee-well.

———o———

THE INDIAN BURIAL-GROUND.
Near Havana, N. Y.

BY H. C. WINTON.

While on this height I stand and gaze
  O'er distant hills and plains around,
One spot I view—a sacred place—
  The Indian Burial-Ground.

That spot which the chieftians of yore—
  Brave men, who have gone to decay—
Most fondly regarded with awe,
  In years that are faded away.

How little the Indian thought
  That the tribes which Catharine led,
So soon would be scattered for aye,
  To join their companions—the dead.

For the red man truly believed,
  When the war-cry ceased to resound,
Manitou would give him a home,
  Beyond the lone Burial-Ground.

And he thought, perhaps, that in time,
  These hills he had hunted around,
A spacious hunting-field would form,
  Encircling the Burial-Ground.

In these happy realms he would roam;
  In these happy realms he would stay;
No sorrow or trouble should come;
  No clouds should obscure endless day.

It was here his fathers were laid,
  And often he viewed yonder mound,
Where the red men slumber in dust,—
  The Indian Burial-Ground.

Then long let their memory live,
  Let their resting place ever be found,
Of the ones who sleep 'neath the sod,
  Within that lone Burial-Ground.

————o————

THE BRIDE OF THE SENECA.

A ROMANCE OF THE GLEN.

BY JOHN WILSON.*

'Tis night—the moon is in the sky—
Low zephyrs through the woodlands sigh;
The autumn foliage, brown and sear,
Tells of the quickly passing year;
No sounds disturb the still repose
Which reigns o'er hill, and vale, and close,

---

*A *nom de plume* of an attache of the Havana *Journal*. Since his impromptu articles, prose as well as poetry, appeared in the *Journal*, he has returned to "merrie England," the land of his birth. In "setting up," the "case" and the "composing stick" were the only MSS. he used.

Save the low murmurs of this Glen,
As leaps its stream from cliff to fen,
List! whence that footstep in the dell—
So light, so stealthily it fell,
It seemed as if a spirit would
Enjoy the sylvan solitude.
Again it falls, more loud and clear,
As to yon bower it draweth near.

* * * * *

This hour Waubuno seeks his bride,
This night he ling'reth at her side,—
O'er hill and flood, o'er plain and vale,
Hath he pursued a winding trail;
Lest some of stern Arouski's braves,
Who dwell by Seneca's dark waves,
Should meet him in his secret way,
Ere the red East proclaims the day.

* * * * *

Within that leafy, emerald bower,
Waoniasea waits the hour
Which to her willing ear will tell
That tale, whose words she loveth well.
At eve she left the wigwam's shade,
And to this dell her footsteps strayed,—
This bower for lovers' converse made,
Shielded by woodland and cascade.
Her father's hate she knoweth well,
Upon her lover it well nigh fell,
When in the thickest of the strife,
Arouski sought Waubuno's life.
And would have slain him, but the day
Was won by the adverse array;
And, on that field her father swore
A deathless hate to him who wore
The plume, red with his warrior's gore.

Taken, by night, in ambush dark,
Waubuno was the arrow's mark.
Carried before his ruthless foe,
The morrow would his death-song know.
That morning came—to him the last—
No more to tread the woodlands vast,
Would Waubuno await the day,
Or share th' exciting chase or fray.
The hour drew near, the warriors round
Assembled on the fatal ground—
The chieftain, nerved to meet his fate,
Stood,—calm, unmoved, erect, sedate.

—But, ere the unerring blow was given—
Ere Waubuno's red crest was riven—
Waoniasea stood between
Him and the tomahawk's dark sheen.
The arm was lower'd that aimed the blow.
Arouski's further will to know.
His daughter to her father clung,
Her lover's life in balance hung,—

Arouski's stoic soul was brave,
His highest aim was glory's grave:
Yet had love's tendrils round that soul
Found genial soil and held control.
Thus when his daughter's tears implored,
He bent to her his soul adored:
Waubuno's forfeit life was spared !
His pledge the ransom'd warrior gave,
No more to wield the bow or glaive
In strife against Arouski's band,
Or tread the Seneca's green strand.

The chief departed—far away
His nation and his wigwam lay.

But, ere he left, Arouski's daughter
With skiff had cross'd the lake's blue water,
And joined Waubuno in the fen
Which lay between the lake and Glen.
And there *another* pledge was made—
What recks it what was thought or said?
What promise given—what words untold,
Affection there did first unfold?

*   *   *   *   *   *

The silver moon has mounted high,
A breeze has risen—o'er the sky
The fleecy clouds begin to fly,
Telling the hour of morning nigh.
—Lo! on the lake's expanse of blue.
Why, at this hour, the birch canoe?

This night Waoniasca meets
Her lover in the wood's retreats—
Those deep retreats of vale and dell,
Which suit Love's oft-told tale so well.
—And hither hath Wabuno come
To bear Arouski's daughter home:
And that her skiff upon the lake,
Fast nearing, now, the Glen's green brake.

*   *   *   *   *

"Waoniasca! if thy flight
Far from thy father's home this night,
Brings to thy bosom one regret—
Turn back—thy footsteps from me set;
Twice in this Glen, in secret, we
Have met, and proved Love's constancy.
For thee I braved thy father's ire;
Now, 'gainst my life his braves conspire;
He heard and knows my love for thee;
He knows my power could set thee free;

If, all unmindful of my vow,
I led my warriors 'gainst him now.
But, if thou art my prize, 'twill be
Through naught save bloodless victory.
No foe of his I now can be—
My life I owe to him, through thee.
And homeward would I rather go
Without thee, than that thou shouldst know
Those pangs which from Repentance flow.
Again I'll track my lonely way
To where my waiting warriors lay.
Now, say what Fate doth bid thee tell—
'I go!' or that dread word 'Farewell!'"

"Nay, my Waubuno!—never!—never!—
Can the blest ties which bind us, sever!
Not though my father's braves appear,
From out each dell and valley sear,
Would I my recent steps retrace,
Or let my love to fear give place.
By the words we here have spoken—
By that promise, still unbroken—
By the love thou made me know,
Hear me—hear me—'I will go!'
Little thou know'st of woman's love,
To think that fear can shake or move
The trust within her heart——
Yes—I go—with thee I go—
To scenes of joy, or scenes of woe;
Fortune's sky or dark or fair,
All thy griefs and joys to share—
Here, beside the cascade's flow,
List me once again—I go!"

*   *   *   *   *

A canoe is on the shore,
   Its paddles idle lay;
She who owned it, now no more
   In that frail light skiff will stray
The Seneca's waters o'er,
   Or around its woodland bay!

   *   *   *   *   *

Gray tints are in the Eastern sky—
Tints which proclaim the sun is nigh:
The lovers onward wend their way
To where Waubuno's warriors lay.
Two hours yet—and he will gain
The thickets of yon woody plain:
There, all secure from boding fears,
His bride may stay her flowing tears.
Two short-lived hours—then the day
Can shine upon them as it may;
For, safe amid his warrior band,
Waubuno dreads no hostile hand.

Hark! whence that sound which echoes o'er
Seneca's now distant shore?
Comes it from Arouski's band?
Yes!—his braves now wield the brand!
Nearer comes the angry sound,
Borne along the valley ground;
Their chief, Arouski, draweth nigh,
Eager th' expectant foe to spy:
On wings of Love and Hate he flies,
A victim, and his child, the prize!

   *   *   *   *   *

   Stern Arouski, in the fray,
      When he raises high the brand,
   No signs of mercy doth betray;
      All must die beneath his hand.

To list the supplicating voice,
    Or stay of life the ebbing sand,
Never was the chieftain's choice.
    *   *   *   *   *

Within a dell, where streaks of day
Peer'd through the leaflet's tinted spray,
Waubuno, wounded—dying—lay!
Arouski's dart had pierced his breast;
And now he wished death as a rest:
'Twould ease the pangs of mortal pain,
'Twas near—his life-blood dyed the plain.

—Waoniasea o'er him bending,
With unavailing care was tending
The wound her father's shaft had ope'd—
And, as she fondly, vainly cop'd
To staunch her lover's welling wound,
She o'er his well-loved form had swooned;
But now Arouski reached the scene,
And peer'd the quivering leaves between—
Then, rushing where his victim lay,
He tore his daughter's form away:
And to the dying chieftain said:

"Waubuno, die! My daughter's arm
Once saved thee from impending harm:
And this return thou mad'st to-day—
Thou wiled her from her home away:
See! now I claim thy dying breath;
I triumph o'er thee in thy death!"
    *   *   *   *   *

Waoniasea watched the sight,
Which closed her lover's soul in night;
Then, in the sternness of despair,
Had vanished every sign of care.

A strange, weird look she gave her sire,
Then viewed the victim of his ire—
And said, in tones which ne'er misgive—
"Naught is now left for which to live."

Arouski's band take up the trail
Which downward leads unto the vale,
Where the Glen looks upon the bay
The warriors left at early day.

Where rolls the torrent down the Glen,
There is a grove—once 'twas a fen.
Above that fen there was a dell—
Waoniasca loved it well.
Here, her Waubuno once had roved
Alone with her his spirit loved.
Here at eve, again she strayed,
While zephyrs through the woodlands played.
—Lo! amid the evening gloom,
She hath found Waubuno's plume!

* * * * *

The soul bereft of Faith and joy,
    Recks not of Hope or Fear:
Its instincts prompt it to destroy
    The spark that ling'reth here—
Bereft of bliss, it seeks for death:
    Seeks it within the lonely cave—
O'er the steep cliff, 'neath the deep wave!

* * * * *

"High is the cliff—yon wave that rolls
Can bring a rest to weary souls!
Not darker is its eddying tide
Than woes which through my bosom glide.
—Ha! see his plume! I know it well—
One moon ago, just here it fell,

When, o'er this ledge, ere yet 'twas day,
He bore me in his arms away.
Hark! whence that voice which thrills my soul?—
Its accents doth my breast condole!
'Tis he! come from the Spirit-land.
Lo! now I see him wave his hand!
List! now again I hear it—"COME!"
—This rock is steep—yet it can close
The record of my withering woes.
In the dark stream which 'neath it flows.
He calls! I'll tempt the flood below:
My loved Waubuno!—watch—I go!"

*   *   *   *   *

There upon the gurgling stream,
    Floats a gory form:
It held a troubled spirit,
    It thrilled to Passion's storm.

Is the blackness of this water
    As dark-hued as her soul,
Who thus dishonored Heaven
    Beneath the torrent's roll?

Speak lightly! ye who blame her:
    Unknown to her the charm
Which Faith brings to the bosom
    When the Evil One would harm..

'Twas the depth of grief which slew her:
    Of mutual love the dearth,—
'Twas a woman's deep affection—
    The purest—best—on earth.

*   *   *   *   *

Remorse will seize thee, guilty Chief!
Thy latest hours are doomed to grief:

Grief, and the demon of Despair,
Shall yet thy heart-strings madly tear :
By thee thy daughter's hopes were crushed,
Her love—her truth—her spirit hushed,
In dark Oblivion's vale—
Waubuno's spectral ghost hath moved
Before thee, wheresoe'er thou roved :
But when the sable form of Death
Requires of thee thy ling'ring breath—
Thy daughter's shapeless corse shall be
Chief phantom of thy misery !

There's a legend that, at midnight hour,
Within the Glen, around the Fall,
And what was once her bower,
Waoniasca and her lover,
In spirit-form are seen to hover :
And o'er the eddying streamlet's hum,
Floats through the air one soft word—"*Come !*"
While high above the torrent's flow
Are heard the answering words—"*I go !*"

JOURNAL OFFICE, Aug. 28, 1867.

——o——

TO SENECA LAKE.

PERCIVAL.

On thy fair bosom, silver lake,
  The wild swan spreads his snowy sail,
And round his breast the ripples break,
  As down he bears before the gale.

On thy fair bosom, waveless stream,
  The dipping paddle echoes far,
And flashes in the moonlight gleam,
  And bright reflects the polar star.

The waves along thy pebbly shore,
  As blows the north wind, heave their foam,
And curl around the dashing oar,
  As late the boatman hies him home.

How sweet, at set of sun, to view
  Thy golden mirror spreading wide;
And see the mist of mantling blue,
  Float round the distant mountain's side.

At midnight hour, as shines the moon,
  A sheet of silver spreads below;
And swift she cuts, at highest noon,
  Light clouds, like wreaths of purest snow.

On thy fair bosom, silver lake,
  O! I could ever sweep the oar,
When early birds at morning wake,
  And evening tells us toil is o'er.

——o——

THE TWO HATS,
IN THE HAVANA GLEN.

BY JOHN WILSON.

Two veritable hats* are here,
  As very plainly does appear:
Here have they been for many a year,
  And will be for many more:

* The two objects known as "The Hats", and which are situated in the bed of the stream in the upper portion of the Glen, are owing to the geological formation of the rock. At a remote period, a "kern," or piece of stone, becoming embedded in the mass, while in a state of fusion, and, subsequently, the rock dividing into two portions, the enclosed kern was broken—thus causing the phenomena of "the hats." Similar objects are found in the Hartz mountains, in Germany.   J. W.

No foolish wight would cheat the rock,
By cutting them from out the block,
Carrying them off at "midnight clock"
　　　T' increase his wardrobe's store.

But, how came this to be their station,
Is food for deep investigation:
What made this rock their situation,
　　　Can any tell?
Perhaps some evil spirit here,
Has counsell'd with a brother seer,
How they could hurt the streamlet clear,
　　　And on it lay a spell—

'Twould damp a woman's curiosity
To seek out the precise velocity;
And tell the depth of animosity,
　　　With which the fiends came down,
Doubtless they "lit" upon their heads,
Which fastened in these rocky beds,
Were burned up by the sun that sheds
　　　Its rays here at high noon:

Or, mayhap, here two "callants" fought,
By purest hatred hither brought;
And, having mutual mischief wrought,
　　　Like the Kilkenny Cats,—
Fighting and fighting, with divers wails,
And making many bloody trails,
Then, in default of genuine *tails*,
　　　Hereon did leave their *Hats*.

But, yet, the truth appears to be,
This is a natural mystery—
One of the many which we see
　　　Spread all around this Glen;

And, like all things beneath the sun,
Once known the wonderment is done;
Once guaged, the mystery has flown—
It puzzles but till—*then*.

———o———

CATHARINE MONTOUR.
THE QUEEN OF THE SENECAS.

BY H. C. WINTON.

"The proudest of all in the hostile array,
Was young Thurenserah, the Dawn of the Day;
The League's Atotarho! the boldest in fight;
The wisest in council! in form the most bright:
The fleetest of foot, the most skilled in the chase,
The glory and boast of the Iroquois race.—STREET.

Queen Catharine formerly resided near McClure's Glen, at Catharinestown (now Havana, N. Y.) Her village was destroyed at the time of Sullivan's Expedition, in 1779.

Long before the Indians had entirely abandoned their favorite hunting-grounds in this region, the hardy pioneers had commenced their settlements.

One of these—probably the first white navigator of Seneca Lake —George Mills, Esq.—was no stranger to the Senecas or Cayugas. His meetings with Catharine Montour and her people were always friendly. Louis Phillippe, while traveling in North America, an exile, was the guest of this pioneer, in his humble log cabin.

At the ceremony of laying the corner stone of The Peoples College, Mr. Mills, although at the advanced age of ninety-four, took an active part, carrying a volume of the Scriptures, while walking in the procession, surrounded by assembled thousands. When he first came to Havana, he found but two families residing in the valley at the head of Seneca Lake. Their neighbors were at Elmira, the Friend's Settlement, and Geneva; at the latter place there was but one log cabin, containing five persons. This pioneer, at the early age of fourteen, had served in the Revolution.

Much concerning Catharine Montour is shrouded in mystery, but the story of her life, connected with that of her people, the Swan-ne-hoh-honts, or Senecas, one of the Six Nations of New York Indians, can never fail to be an interesting one.

The Iroquois, or Six Nations, embraced in their domain the beautiful lakes and streams of the Empire State, many of which still retain their simple aboriginal names.

While contemplating the history of this singular race, we must admit, in the language of Street, that we find " one more melancholy instance of a once powerful and happy people entirely disappearing from the face of the earth;" and also to quote from the writings of Stone, the eminent Indian Biographer, "the Indians have had no writer to relate their own side of the story."

At some time, kind reader, perchance you have been
To a wild rocky dell, now called McClure's Glen,
With its caverns and cliffs, and o'erhanging trees,
Whose branches keep time with the sweet summer breeze ;
To approach and behold the varied delights,
Here, with exquisite charms, all Nature invites ;
In silence we gaze where the wild waters foam,
Enraptured in thought as enchanted we roam.
—Not far from this spot, as traditions relate,
The red men once held their rude councils of state ;
Though simple their habits, their friendships were pure,
And the queen of the tribe, was Cath'rine Montour ;
And when Sullivan came, as conquerors come,
With the shrill-sounding fife, and roll of the drum :
'Twas here she then dwelt—fair queen of the valley—
The pride of the red men who round her would rally.

The smoke of her wigwam no longer is seen,
And the war dance is held no more on the green :
The hills with wild war cries no longer resound ;
Her braves are now sleeping in yon grassy mound ;
And of that lone spot a few thoughts I would write—

So help me, my muse, in the words I indite;
For the red men rest near the pale faces there,
With Ilah–wen–ne–yoh, now, they're free from earth's care;
And there in the morn, Jis–ko–ko doth sing
Sweet carolling notes, foreteller of Spring;
While Seneca Inlet, still, murmuring stream,
Flows gently along; it disturbs not the dream
Of those who there sleep, near the green, grassy shore,
Departed from earth, to return—nevermore.

But, now of the red men few traces remain,
Who so freely once roamed o'er hill and o'er plain;
And all who here knew them are passing away,
For ev'rything earthly soon goes to decay,—
Like the frost of the morn, 'neath autumn's bright sun,
Our brief lives are ended when scarce they've begun;
But, yet, there was one—can you guess who I mean?
But a few years since was his aged form seen:
Light were his footsteps as he came from the hills,
For most hearty and hale was FATHER GEORGE MILLS.
The sons of the woods he had known long and well,
And of former days many tales he could tell,
Of wild hunting sports, in happy days of yore,
When the streams were dipt with the Indian's oar.

Some who read these lines, perhaps may remember,.
A beautiful day, ere the ides of September—
Eighteen fifty-eight, I believe, was the year,
When such a vast concourse of people were here
To witness a scene most impressive and grand;
There came many wise men from over the land;
For the corner stone of a College was laid,
While thousands of people around were arrayed.
In the pioneer's hands the dearly prized page—
It had cheered him in youth, and solaced in age;

Tho' whitened his locks, and tho' worn was his frame,
In the ev'ning of life, naught caring for fame,
A tear in his eye, as he marched in the line,
He was thinking, perhaps, of a bygone time,
When he came, in his youth, to this beautiful vale
With no road or path, save the Seneca's trail;
When few were the people, the dwellings but *two*,
From the river Chemung, to yon lake of blue;
When the bear and the wolf in the forest held sway;
No wonder that he should have wept on that day;
Or, perhaps he thought of the one who had shared
His early life's care—she taken, he spared—
The light of his home in the wilderness free,
A daughter of Erin, sweet Isle of the Sea.
But now the "Master" of all, hath called him on high,
For, Free and Accepted, his time came to die.
Hereabouts he dwelt, some threescore years or more,
Gladly welcoming all who came to his door:
And once to his cabin he welcomed a king,—
A prince of proud France—'twas an uncommon thing.

But, still, in the distance yon fair lake remains,
Sweet mem'rys recalling of Percival's strains;
And many love tales have been echoed, I ween,
O'er its light sparkling waves of glittering sheen;
For its tranquil bosom of clear azure blue,
Often has borne the young warrior's canoe.
—Most beautiful lake! thou art ever the same,
As when Seneca braves to thee gave their name;
May thy crystal waters, so placid and pure,
Keep long in remembrance the name of MONTOUR;
For here the Great Spirit, for purposes wise,
First gave to her people a home 'neath the skies:
'Mid the glens and cascades, which so thickly abound,
Where the student of Nature so often is found.

Now there *are* some things we would ask thee, fair queen,
Couldst thou but return, to the valley's bright green;
And besides, I would know—if thou canst me tell—
In the bright Spirit Land, with thy tribe, is it well?
And then, to recede from that echoless shore,
To the regions of earth returning once more,
Perhaps you might tell us if *time* has much changed
The hills and the plains where *your* warriors ranged;
For the wild deer is seen no more on the hill,
And long has the horn of the hunter been still ;
Through the valley is laid a strong iron band,
O'er which the swift engine flies fast through the land.
Now here is one thing many people would learn,
Tradition has brought; the tale shall we spurn ?
That where yonder vast marsh now flames ev'ry year ;
Well—I *would* that one of your chieftains were here,
Perhaps he might tell us where'bouts was the *spring*,
That *salt* might be made, for great riches 'twould bring;
And this was a secret—not many knew where,
This Indian treasure was guarded with care;
And besides, there are some who gladly would know,
If "rock oil" abounds in the regions below;
For as strange as it seems—I *will* be quite plain—
Many men here'bouts, have had "oil on the brain."
And of what were the teeth*—what animal rare,
That were found in the vale? and whence came they there?
—Near the wild wooded glen, where bloom the wild flowers,
In your time were the fields of Phinehas Bowers;
Once or twice since then the domain has changed hands,
Until huge brick walls now adorn the wide lands,
And these massive walls are the Peoples College,
Conceived by lovers of art and of knowledge;

---

* These curious specimens—relics of the Mastodon *Maximus*, were found
some years since, while excavations were being made, on the lands of the late
Hon. Chas. Cook. The writer is rather inclined to the opinion that several of
them are at present preserved in the State Cabinet of Natural History.

Where the rich and the poor united may stand,
Where science and labor may join hand in hand.
—You remember the Falls on the west hillside,
She-qua-gah, so long of our valley the pride;
Where Sa-go-yea-wa-tha* in route from the lake,
Toned his clarion voice—"the keeper awake."
And Aunt Sarah's Falls firmly stand as of yore,
O'er which the white waters unceasingly pour;
And though the old land-marks are fast growing few,
The *cold spring* yet remains—near lock number *two*.

You will see by this that we cherish your fame,
Two townships in Schuyler from you take their name;
MONTOUR is the younger, and near by is seen,
Her fair older sister—the town of CATHARINE;
And another fond link, adds strength to the chain,
'Tis on yon hillside, rising high o'er the plain,
Where the ones we have loved, lie silent and cold;
Their joys are all number'd, their sorrows all told—
In remembrance of thee, fair Indian maid,
We have named the lov'd spot, where our dear ones are laid;
And there, we yet hope a proud column will rise,
Proclaiming your worth—pointing up to the skies.

And now Forest Maiden, we bid thee adieu,
With Hah-wen-ne-yoh rest, Sa-ha-wee† so true;
While our beautiful lakes and streams shall endure,
Will be cherish'd the name of Cath'rine Montour.
Then sleep A-to-tar-ho, thy warriors brave,
Like thee Thurenserah, sleep low in the grave;

---

* Red Jacket. It is a well authenticated fact, that this distinguished Seneca Chief and orator frequently visited She-qua-gah, "the place of the roaring waters," for practice to increase the volume of his eloquent voice. His Indian name signified "the keeper awake."

† This word signifies in the language of the Iroquois, "a vine," and was also, sometimes used by them as a term of affection or endearment.

On the wave's white crest laving Seneca's shore,
No more will be seen thy light-feather'd oar,
Thy proud Swan–ne–ho–honts, once powerful race,
Skannadario's* shores, will never more trace ;
Their batteaux no more on Cataraqui† ride,
As in days that are gone, when thou wert their pride ;
Though thy braves never more may darken the plain,
Though here their wild war-songs be heard not again :
Yet sleep Thurenserah—the Dawn of the Day—
When Hah–wen–ne–yoh calls, we too, must obey.

———o———

AUTUMN IN THE GLEN.

BY JOHN WILSON.

The fading leaves are falling now—
　　The Glen survives its flowers—
While o'er it sweeps the moaning winds
　　Of Autumn's gloomy hours:
Its summer hues are fading fast,
　　Like hearts which outlive their joy—
And soon will come stern winter's blast
　　Its glories to destroy.

Around its grey, rock-bound confines
　　October clouds career,—
The torent's dirge—the groaning pine—
　　Bewail the fleeting year.
With rushing and impetuous sweep
　　Over the cliffs sublime,
That gurg'ling torrent rolls Its course
　　Like Life—the Sea of Time !

* Lake Ontario.
† The River St. Lawrence.

A leaf—a sear and wither'd leaf—
  Falls on the rushing spray:
The waters bear it on their breast,
  Over the rocks away:—
Thus life bears on its eddying wave
  Griefs—hopes—joys—it hath seen—
Leaving no vestige in its course
  That such have ever been.

Ye torrents! LIFE and TIME!
  Ye own no tarrying spot below!
Still flowing where the the past hath flown,
  Still flowing—and to flow!
Thus doth yon stream tumultuous flow
  O'er rocks and grottoes brown—
O'er cliffs—past overhanging woods—
  Down the last Cascade, down.

Its fateful page the waning year
  Hath silently unroll'd:
Its joy and sorrow, hope and fear,
  Past—like a tale long told!
And leaves it on Faitn's brow the while,
  No trace of buried care?
Oh, but for Hope—her word and smile—
  What furrows had been there!

So, in this Glen, where late hath bloomed
  Fair Summer's flow'ry sheen,
The many-tinted leaves now fall
  The rust'ling boughs between.
But Spring will yet restore each leaf—
  The flowers will bloom again,—
And Earth forget her transient grief
  'Mid Summer's gentle reign.

THE PEOPLES COLLEGE.

"Another Temple to the Architect above."—WALLACE.

Respectfully inscribed to the patrons and friends of the Masonic School and Asylum, at Havana, N. Y.

BY H. C. WINTON.

All hail! thou mammoth pile
Of brick, and stone, and lime,
Wherefore so high doth reach
Your columns and your walls?
It almost seems as if
You were a thing of life,
So rapid have you grown.
Methinks for some wise end
You were conceived and built;
And what is that, now tell?
'Twas not for palace—no—
Commerce—no; nor war:
What then! ah, now I know,
A modern temple, where
Art and labor shall combine;
To form the perfect man;
Within whose stately halls
The student toils to reach
The goal of earthly fame,
With wisdom's honors crowned.

But why unite the two?
For what good reason now
Should lofty science bow,
Linked hand in glove with toil?
Wherefore unite with classic lore,
Mechanic hand or plowman's arm?
And dost thou then not know
That this the age demands,
A people now are great

As knowledge guides their hands.
"Old things have passed away,"
The times have greatly changed,
And he who would be great
Must be a working man.

By this, I do not mean
That 'twas not always thus;
It would be wrong to say,
No true great man has ever lived,
Who did not work, and often hard.
The sense in which I mean
Is this, that any branch of art
In which you would excel,
Or trade, or occupation,
Should be known and well,
In practice and in theory.

But whence this idea ?
And from where did it come ?
Let me tell you the name
Of this edifice grand ;
When perhaps you can guess,
What gives to this scheme
Such a wonderful zest,
'Tis—The Peoples College,
And among its best friends,
Of rank and of station,
Are lovers of knowledge,
Hard working, self-made men,
The pulse of the nation.
And when one such you find,
Which you can easy do,
You'll meet a friend to art
And healthy labor, too.

And kindred ones there are
Who, striving to erect
A monument to time—
A present and a future good—
Now watch with eager eye
The progress of these walls.

'Twas of such men as these
That a Washington came—
A Franklin and Webster—
And hosts of others, too,
We can not forget them;
They will be remembered
While America lasts,
Or a Europe endures.
Their cause was their country,
Their prayers for her good;
That cause may it last,
Those pray'rs be revered,
While a nation stands forth
To present to the world
A banner of freedom,
Aye, forever unfurl'd—
Supported by science,
Genial labor and art;
With these, together joined,
Oh who can then foretell
The future of our land.

And now, before I leave the theme,
Your indulgence I ask, and that you
With favor will regard the scheme;
And should you chance to see a youth,
Perhaps, a wand'ring orphan boy,
To whom you'd lend a helping hand.

Along the stormy path of life ;
It may be then, you'll not forget
To point him to the Peoples College,
Where he may learn to walk aright—
May learn some useful calling,
Where he may gather wisdom's fruits
To store away for future needs.

For such a noble cause as this
In which all are interested,
May it be hoped that you
Will give at least, if nothing more—
Your earnest, kind, good wishes ?
But, if with fortune you are blest,
Remember, funds are still required,
And legacies are not refused ;
(In fact they're really needed ;)
While small amounts for one great end,
Together, make a vast account ;
As sparkling rills and rippling streams,
The sweeping, mighty river form.

In such a work, to be enrolled,
'Twere worthy king or bishop,
To be engaged in doing good,
Should be our high ambition ;
For he who strives to aid the young,
Ascending in the paths of truth,
Fulfills a heavenly mission.
In Sacred Writ these words are said,
To them we should give earnest heed ;—
Upon the waters cast thy bread,
And after many days have flown,
To thee, perchance, it may return.

Thus while the student step by step,
Cheer'd by your gracious smile,
A kindly word—a helping hand,
Is toiling up the rugged height,
Where fame and honor hold their sway,
In the golden realms of knowledge;
He will look back and bless the day
That formed the PEOPLES COLLEGE.

---o---

THE CAVE OF THE ECHOES.
IN THE HAVANA GLEN.

BY JOHN WILSON.

Echoing—echoing—echoing ever,
The silv'ry-tinted pearl-drops sever
  A way through the rifted rock.
    Echoing—echoing—with ceaseless flow,
    Adown their wave-worn path they go.

Echoing—echoing—echoing ever,
What do the echoes say?—
  They tell of the Past, its changes vast,
  And the ages flown away;
    Echoing—echoing—with ceaseless flow,
    Over the rocky ledge they go.

Dripping, dripping, dripping,
  Noiselessly they flow;—
    Flowing, flowing, flowing,
    Into the dell below:
      Then, o'er the cascade wildly dashing,
      Over the emerald valley splashing.
      In the golden sunbeams flashing.

Echoing,—echoing—echoing,
With a tinkling, liquid sound;
    Echoing, echoing, ever
    The cavernous vault around;

Gliding, gliding, gliding,
  Like the Past to Eternity's shore:
Vanishing, vanishing, vanishing,
  Like mist on the mountain's hoar.

Mingling, mingling, mingling,
With the drops which have gone before;
  Like the hopes and fears
  Of the buried years,
    · That are gone for evermore:
    Or like the graves
    'Neath the ocean's waves,
Which the heedless billows travel o'er,
Where the sea-bird's tireless pinions soar.

Echoing, echoing, day by day,
The echoes tune their ceaseless lay,
  Singing to the leafy dale
  As the zephyrs fan the vale,
  Keeping time with plaintive wail:
Echoing, echoing, when the night
Claims the moonbeam's softer light;—
  Never ceasing, never ending,
  To the morn their music lending,
  With the eve their cadence blending,
Thro' the night their soft notes sending.

Echoing, echoing, echoing,
Flowing, flowing, flowing,
  *   *   · *   *   *

  Dashing, dashing, dashing,
    *   *   *   *   *

  Flashing, flashing, flashing,
    *   *   *   *   *

      Down the drops go
      With endless flow   ·
    Thro' valley, cave, grotto and all.
    Over the Glen's last Water-fall.
Montour House, 4th Sept., 1867.